MERCER MAYER'S
LC + THE CRITTER KIDS®

THE
PIZZA WAR

A Golden Book • New York

Western Publishing Company, Inc., Racine, Wisconsin 53404

A Mercer Mayer Ltd./J. R. Sansevere Book

Library of Congress Catalog Card Number: 94-75364
ISBN: 0-307-15979-5/ISBN: 0-307-65979-8 (lib. bdg.)   A MCMXCV

Written by Erica Farber/J. R. Sansevere

LC

VELVET

LITTLE SISTE

TIGER

KOOL BEAR

SLICK RICK

SU SU   GABBY   TIMOTHY

GATOR   FLEX   HENRIETTA

CHAPTER 1

THE LEANING TOWER OF PIZZA

The pizza war started on a Friday afternoon. LC was in social studies, his last class of the day, counting the minutes till the weekend began.

Mr. Hogwash, the teacher, picked up the textbook that lay open on his desk. "And now to continue our study of the Middle Ages," he said, "turn to page 27 in your textbooks."

LC turned to page 27. There was a picture of a strange-looking building.

Suddenly a note landed on his desk. He opened it carefully.

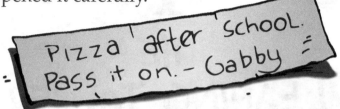

Pizza after school. Pass it on. - Gabby

Cool, thought LC. Pizza was his favorite food. And the best place to get pizza in Critterville was Tony's Pizzeria. LC looked toward the front of the room. Mr. Hogwash had his back to the class. He was pointing to something on the map.

LC looked to his left.

"Pssst!" LC whispered to Tiger.

Tiger looked up from his book. LC aimed and threw the note onto Tiger's desk. Tiger opened the note and looked at LC. Then he gave him the thumbs-up signal.

LC couldn't wait to go to Tony's. His mouth watered just thinking about Tony's cheesy pizza with its chewy crust. LC started drawing a picture of a pizza.

"What is one of the most famous towers of medieval times?" Mr. Hogwash asked.

He looked around the room and then walked down the aisle toward LC.

LC was busy adding pepperoni and extra cheese to his picture. He didn't notice Mr. Hogwash standing by his desk.

"Mr. Critter?" said Mr. Hogwash, bending over him. "What have we here?" he asked, grabbing the drawing off LC's desk.

"Pizza?" said LC with a grin.

The whole class looked at him and started to laugh. How did Mr. Hogwash always know when he wasn't paying attention? thought LC.

"Actually, Mr. Critter, you're right, although your pronunciation is not correct," said Mr. Hogwash.

"I am?" LC said, looking up at Mr. Hogwash in surprise.

"Yes," said Mr. Hogwash. "One of the most famous towers built during medieval times is called the Leaning Tower of Pisa. But it is pronounced '*pee*-za,' not '*peet*-za.'" Mr. Hogwash crumpled up LC's drawing and dropped it on his desk. "Now, does anyone know why the tower leans?"

Timothy held up his hand. "Actually, the tower started leaning before it was even finished. The foundation wasn't strong enough."

"Precisely," said Mr. Hogwash. "And it is all because of this accident that the town of Pisa is so well-known today."

Just then the bell rang. "Pizza time!" LC shouted.

Everyone laughed again.

"Class dismissed," said Mr. Hogwash. "See you on Monday."

Everyone ran down the hallway to their lockers.

"So you guys are coming, right?" asked Gabby, turning around.

"Definitely," LC said.

"We are, too," said Velvet and Henrietta from across the hall.

"Ready?" said Su Su, her new pink cowboy boots making a thumping sound as she walked up to Gabby. "We better hurry if we want to get a good table."

"Yeah," said Velvet. "I heard a lot of the

older kids are going to be there."

"It's the grand opening," said Gabby.

"Grand opening?" said LC. "But Tony's has always been there."

"Tony's?" all the Critter Kids said, turning and staring at LC.

"Yeah," said LC. "Aren't we going to Tony's to get pizza?"

"No way," said Su Su. "We're going to Presto Pizza. It's the coolest."

"You'll love it, dude," said Tiger.

"But we always go to Tony's," said LC.

"Well, it's time for something new," Gabby said.

LC followed his friends down the steps. If everybody wanted to go to Presto Pizza, he would go, too. But he was sure Tony's pizza was still the best.

CHAPTER 2

NEW PLACE IN TOWN

When LC and the Critter Kids got to Presto Pizza, the place was packed. There were streamers and balloons hanging from the ceiling, and a big jukebox in one corner. Waiters and waitresses were gliding between the tables on roller skates.

"Isn't this the coolest?" said Gabby as they all sat down in a big booth.

"Yeah," said Su Su. "Totally."

"But it doesn't seem like a real pizza place," LC said. "It doesn't even smell like pizza."

"Give me a break," said Gabby. "Presto is the pizza place of the future."

"But what about the pizza?" LC asked. "I bet it doesn't taste as good as Tony's."

"So what?" said Gabby. "We're not here for the food. We're here for the atmosphere."

LC picked up the menu. It was in the shape of a jukebox.

"I'm going to get the Purple Pizza Eater," announced Henrietta, chewing the ice from her water glass. "I'm starved."

"What is it?" asked Velvet.

"I don't know," said Henrietta. "I just like the color purple."

A waitress skated over to their booth. The lights went out and a spotlight shone on the waitress as music began to play. The waitress twirled around on her skates, singing, *"Some folks may want to put Presto down."* A group of waiters and waitresses chimed in: *"Down, down."*

"They only do it 'cuz we're new in town," the waitress continued.

"'Cuz we're new, 'cuz we're new in town," sang the group.

The waitress opened her arms wide as she sang, *"So why don't you give us a try, and you'll be sure to find out why . . ."*

The group joined in, *"Presto Pizza . . . leader of the pizza pack. Vroom, vroom, vroom."*

As the last *"vroom"* was sung, the lights came back on.

"Can I take your order?" the waitress asked, blowing a big pink bubble with her gum.

"I'll have the Chantilly," said Gabby.

Everybody ordered something different. But LC didn't know what to get. He didn't see a regular old slice of pepperoni pizza listed anywhere on the menu.

"I don't want anything," he said.

"There's a three dollar minimum," the waitress said. "So whaddya want?"

LC was getting mad. He didn't want to be at Presto Pizza in the first place. He didn't care how cool it was.

"Whaddya want, kid?" the waitress said again. "I don't have all day."

"Nothing," said LC. "I'm leaving."

"Suit yourself," she said, skating away.

"You can't leave," said Gabby. "We just got here."

"Oh, yes I can," said LC.

"Where are you going?" Gabby asked.

"To the best pizza place in Critterville," said LC.

CHA**3**TER

NOT ENOUGH DOUGH

When LC got to Tony's, there were no other customers there. He hopped on a stool in front of the counter and spun around, just like he always did.

LC took a deep sniff. It sure smelled good—the way a pizza place was supposed to smell. Maybe it didn't have a fancy jukebox and roller-skating waitresses who sang, but it had one thing that Presto would never have—Tony.

"LC, how ya doin'?" asked Tony, wiping his hands on his stained white apron.

◀ 12 ▶

"Long time no see."

"Hey, Tony," LC said. "Did your wife have the baby yet?"

"No," Tony said. "Any day now. Any day."

Just then the door opened and a guy in a suit walked in. "Where's my pizza?" he asked.

"It's coming right up," said Tony.

Tony opened the oven and slid out a pizza. He sprinkled some extra cheese and some spices over the top and then slid it back into the oven.

"Listen, I don't have all day," said the guy. "It's bad enough that you don't deliver."

"Hey, do you think Leonardo da Critter painted the ceiling of the Sistine Chapel in five minutes?" said Tony. "Good pizza takes time. Right, LC?"

"Yep," said LC.

Tony opened the oven and took out the pizza. He slid it into a box and sliced it. "Ten dollars and fifty cents," Tony said, ringing up the sale.

"Oh, no, I only have a ten," said the guy, reaching into his pocket and pulling out a ten dollar bill.

"That's okay," said Tony. "Forget about it."

"Thanks," said the guy. He picked up his pizza and walked out the door.

"So, LC, what do you want?" asked Tony. "The usual?"

LC nodded. He watched as Tony picked up a slice and put cheese on top, and then

pepperoni all over. Just the way LC liked it.

LC licked his lips, waiting for his slice. Just then the phone rang. Tony picked it up. At the same moment the door banged open. LC turned around. He couldn't believe his eyes. It was the Critter Kids!

"Yummy," Henrietta said. "Real pizza."

"What are *you* doing here?" asked LC.

"The pizza at Presto's was terrible," said Gabby, sitting down next to LC.

"Yeah," said Tiger. "It was the worst."

"You can't do that!" Tony suddenly yelled into the phone. "It's Friday night— how am I supposed to come up with that kind of money? That's not right!"

LC frowned. What did Tony need money for? he wondered.

"Or you'll what?" Tony exploded. "My father started this business before you were born. You can't do that!"

LC and Gabby stared at each other. None of the Kids knew what was going on.

Tony slammed down the phone.

"Is something wrong?" LC asked.

"The bank is closing me down," Tony said, "unless I come up with the money I owe them by next Monday."

"They can't do that," said LC. "Everybody loves Tony's Pizzeria."

"Not anymore," said Tony. "Not with that fancy-shmancy Presto Pizza in town."

Tony took LC's slice out of the oven and put it in front of him. It was just the way LC liked it—the pepperoni was crispy and the cheese was all goopey and melted.

"So, kids," said Tony, trying to smile. "Slices for everyone?"

The Critter Kids nodded.

"Let me guess," Tony said. "Henrietta wants everything. Tiger and Gator want pepperoni, Gabby and Su Su want plain,

Velvet wants mushrooms, and Timothy wants anchovies. Am I right?"

"Yep," said the Critter Kids.

When Tony went into the kitchen, Gabby motioned for everybody to get into a huddle. "Let's meet at the clubhouse tomorrow morning," Gabby said. "We've got to come up with a plan to help Tony."

"Yeah," said LC.

They all agreed there had to be something they could do.

CHAPTER 4

SPECIAL DELIVERY

The next morning LC woke up feeling hungry. He decided he'd have a huge bowl of Crispy Crispers with a lot of milk. He got dressed and went downstairs to the kitchen. Little Sister was already up, sitting in her chair at the table. She was pouring milk over her cereal.

"Hey, you're using all the milk," LC said.

"Yep," said Little Sister. "I like my cereal mushy, not crunchy, so I need a lot of milk."

"But now there's none for

me," said LC.

Just then the kitchen doorbell rang. LC walked over to the screen door. It was Mr. McCoy from the Critterville Creamery.

"You forgot to leave your empties in the box again," said Mr. McCoy. "Here's your milk for the week." He handed LC two big bottles.

"Perfect timing," said LC, taking the bottles. Then he handed Mr. McCoy the empties. "Thanks, Mr. McCoy," he said.

Mr. McCoy tipped his hat and smiled. "Have a good day," he said.

LC put one bottle in the refrigerator and opened the other one. "Just in time," said LC, pouring milk over his cereal. "Mr. McCoy delivered the milk just in time . . ."

Suddenly LC jumped up. "That's it!" he shouted. "We can deliver pizzas!"

"What are you yelling about?" asked Little Sister.

"Never mind," said LC. "I've got to go to the clubhouse for an important meeting."

"What about your cereal?" asked Little Sister, eyeing LC's full bowl.

"You can have it," said LC. He ran out the kitchen door.

He got to the clubhouse just as Gabby came running across the backyard. They went inside and sat down at the table. LC couldn't wait to tell everyone his plan.

A few minutes later Tiger and Gator showed up, followed by Velvet, Su Su, Timothy, and Henrietta.

"Order, order, the meeting to save Tony's Pizzeria is now in order," said Gabby. "Does anyone have any suggestions?"

"I have a great idea," LC said.

"What?" said Henrietta, taking a big bite of her egg and bacon sandwich.

"We can all deliver pizzas on the weekends," said LC. "As soon as everyone knows Tony's is delivering, he'll do tons of business."

"I second that idea," said Gabby. "All those in favor, raise their hands."

Everyone raised their hands except for Henrietta.

"Henrietta, do you have an objection?" asked Gabby.

"Yeah," said Henrietta, bits of bacon sticking out of the corners of her mouth. "I have an objection. This sandwich—they forgot the jelly."

"All right," Gabby said. "LC and I will go down to Tony's first to tell him our plan. Tiger and Gator, you get your bikes for the deliveries. And Timothy, you go get your calculator so we can add up how much money we're collecting."

"What should we do?" asked Henrietta, pointing at herself and Velvet.

"You two should go spy on Presto Pizza and see how many customers they have," said Gabby.

"Spy?" said Velvet, her eyes widening.

"Yes, spy," Gabby said. "This is a war. And the best way to win is to know exactly what your enemy is doing."

"Yeah!" said LC. He wasn't sure what Gabby was talking about, but it sure sounded good.

LC and Gabby got to Tony's just as Tony flipped the CLOSED sign to OPEN.

"Right on time," LC said to Tony.

"You want another slice already?" Tony asked.

"No, thanks," said LC.

"Actually, we're here to help you," said Gabby. "We want to deliver pizzas on the weekends."

"Why?" asked Tony.

"So you can make more money to pay back the bank," said LC.

Tony scratched his chin and smiled.

"Please, Tony," said Gabby. "Just give us a try. We'll be the best delivery kids ever."

"Yeah, Tony," said LC.

"You guys will do it for free?" asked Tony.

"Of course," said Gabby. "We really want to help you out."

"Okay," said Tony. "It's a deal. And I'll even show you how to make pizza."

"All right!" yelled LC.

They all shook hands.

Tony showed them how to grate the cheese, stir the sauce, and how to knead the pizza dough. LC and Gabby watched Tony spin a pizza on the tips of his fingers and then throw it up in the air. He caught it perfectly. Then Tony showed them how he slid the pizzas in and out of the oven.

"Wow!" said LC.

"My father taught me to make pizza the same way he learned how to in the old country," said Tony. "He could make a crust that would melt in your mouth."

Just then the phone rang and Tony picked it up. "Tony's," he said. He pulled the pen from behind his ear and began writing. "So that's two large pies with anchovies, mushrooms, and green peppers. Okay. You can pick them up in—"

"We'll deliver them," LC said, jumping up and down.

"I mean, they'll be delivered in twenty minutes," said Tony.

LC and Gabby helped Tony put the toppings on the pizzas. When they were ready, Tony slid them into two big red-and-white cardboard boxes. He wrote the address on the top box. LC noticed that it was right near his house.

"Sure you can carry them?" asked Tony.

"No problem," said Gabby. "We'll be right back."

LC picked up one pizza and Gabby picked up the other. They walked down the block and around the corner. The big boxes were hot and a little awkward. After a few blocks, LC's arms started to hurt a little.

After another block, Gabby stopped.

"Can we take a break?" she asked.

LC and Gabby put their pizzas down on

a parked car. Suddenly the car started and pulled away from the curb.

"Stop!" yelled LC, running after the car. "You've got our pizzas!"

The car stopped at the traffic light. The pizzas slid off the car and landed on the sidewalk. LC and Gabby ran over to them. The boxes looked okay—a little squashed, but not too bad.

LC and Gabby picked up the boxes and kept walking.

"I wonder who's getting these pizzas," said Gabby.

LC looked at the address on the box and then at the address on the mailbox in front of them. "Oh, no," he said.

"What's the matter?" asked Gabby.

"You'll never believe who ordered these pizzas," said LC.

"Who?" said Gabby.

Just then the door to the house opened. "Finally," a voice croaked. "Tony said

twenty minutes and it's been exactly twenty-two minutes and twelve seconds." Mrs. Crabtree walked out onto her porch. She was wearing her meanest frown.

"Sorry it took so long, Mrs. Crabtree," said LC. "Here are the pies you ordered."

"Hope you like 'em," said Gabby.

Gabby and LC handed the pizzas to Mrs. Crabtree. She opened the boxes and inspected each pizza. There was cheese and anchovies stuck to the tops of the boxes.

"Here's your money," Mrs. Crabtree said. "But tell Tony next time I want my anchovies on the pizza, not on the box." Then she closed her front door with a loud bang, right in Gabby and LC's faces.

"I know we'll do better next time," LC said.

"Yeah," said Gabby. "Hey, we better get back to Tony's. He probably has a ton of new deliveries by now."

LC and Gabby ran back to the pizzeria. Everyone was there except for Velvet and Henrietta.

"What's taking them so long?" Gabby asked.

"Maybe they got captured," said Tiger.

"That's ridiculous," said Gabby as the door opened and Henrietta and Velvet walked in.

"Where have you been?" Gabby asked, her hands on her hips. "And what is all that stuff?" she added, pointing at Henrietta.

"All that spying really gave me an appetite," said Henrietta, taking a big bite of her triple scoop ice cream cone and popping a potato chip in her mouth at the same time.

"Well?" said Gabby. "What did you find out?"

"The place was packed," said Henrietta.

"Totally," said Velvet, nodding her head. "And they kept sending guys out with deliveries, too."

"Oh, no," said Gabby. "That's just what I was afraid of."

"Don't worry," said LC. "I'm sure we'll have lots of deliveries, too. It's still early."

For the rest of the day, LC and the Critter Kids grated cheese, mopped the floor, cleaned the tables, and washed the dishes. There were some customers, but the pizza place was never full. Worse than that, the phone never rang.

"I'm sure somebody will call," LC kept saying.

But no one did.

DON'T BE A MEATBALL

LC worried about Tony all weekend and all through school on Monday. He wished there was more they could do.

After school LC was standing in front of his locker. Gabby was at her locker, too, packing up her books.

"Hey, dude," said Tiger, walking over to LC. "What's up?"

"I was just thinking about Tony," said LC.

"Me too," said Gabby.

"Me three,"added Gator.

"What are you guys talking about?"

asked Su Su as she and the rest of the Critter Kids walked up to them.

"About Tony," said LC. "If only everybody in Critterville knew that Tony might go out of business."

"Yeah," said Henrietta. "Then they'd remember how good his pizza is and how bad Presto's is."

"That's it!" said Gabby.

"Huh?" said LC.

"We'll advertise," said Gabby. "We'll make up flyers telling all about Tony's delicious homemade pizza and his new weekend delivery service."

"That's a great idea," said LC.

"I can do the flyers on my computer," said Timothy. "We can even put in a picture of Tony, if we want."

"Cool," said LC.

"Do you have your camera with you, Timothy?" asked Gabby.

Timothy nodded and took his camera out of his briefcase. "It's a Polaroid," said Timothy, handing it to Gabby. "That way the picture will come out right away."

"LC and I will take the picture," said Gabby. "You guys start working on what the flyer is going to say. We'll meet you at Timothy's in half an hour."

Gabby and LC ran down the hallway and out of the building. They didn't stop running until they got to Tony's.

"Tony, Tony," said Gabby and LC together.

"What? What?" Tony asked.

"We need to take your picture," said LC.

"For what?" asked Tony.

"For the flyers we're making," said Gabby.

"Picture? Flyers?" repeated Tony, looking from LC to Gabby. "What are you kids talking about?"

"See, we're making up these flyers advertising your pizza and your new weekend delivery service," said Gabby.

"And we're going to put them up all over Critterville," LC added.

"So we want your picture to be on the flyer," said Gabby. "See what we mean?"

Tony nodded. "You kids never quit, huh?"

"Nope," said Gabby. "You know what they say—'Quitters never win.' Or is it 'Winners never quit'?"

LC picked up the camera and waited for Gabby to get Tony ready. First she made Tony change his apron. Then she had him stand in front of the counter. Then she had him stand behind the counter. Then she

made him throw a pizza up in the air. Then she had him smile. Then she had him look serious. LC started getting impatient.

"Gabby, we're running out of time," said LC. "You better hurry up."

Finally Gabby had Tony stand in front of the counter, pointing to a whole stack of pizzas, with a big smile on his face. LC took the last picture.

"This looks great," said LC as the picture came out of the camera. "See you later," LC said to Tony.

"See you," said Gabby.

Tony just smiled and shook his head as LC and Gabby flew out the door. When they got to Timothy's, the rest of the Critter Kids were in his bedroom, gathered around his computer.

"Here's the picture," said Gabby.

Timothy scanned it into the computer. Then he made the picture fit at the top of the flyer, right above the words.

"Okay, guys, we're ready to print," said Timothy.

"Cool," said LC.

Timothy flipped a switch on his printer and within seconds the first flyer came out.

Su Su took the flyer from the printer tray.

"It looks awesome," said Tiger.

"Totally," agreed Su Su.

"Let me see it," said Gabby, looking over Su Su's shoulder.

LC ran over to see it, too. The flyer did look pretty good, even if he said so himself. Especially the picture.

Over the next three days the Critter Kids put up flyers on telephone poles, bulletin boards, and lampposts all over Critterville. By Thursday night there were flyers everywhere.

On Friday morning LC met Gabby by his mailbox. They started walking to school.

"I know the flyers are going to work," said Gabby. "I just have this feeling."

"Yeah," said LC.

"Hey," said Gabby as they passed the lamppost at the end of their street. "I know I put a flyer on that post."

"I know you did, too," said LC. "I was with you."

"So what happened to it?" asked Gabby.

"I don't know," said LC.

The two of them walked a few more

blocks. Suddenly LC stopped at a telephone pole.

"Hey," he said. "I know I put a flyer up here yesterday, and now it's gone."

"There's got to be an explanation," said Gabby. "This is too weird."

Just then they saw Mrs. Crabtree up ahead. She was yelling at some guy and hitting him over the head with her purse. LC and Gabby hurried to see what was going on.

"You're not supposed to do that!" Mrs. Crabtree yelled, hitting the guy, who was wearing a Presto Pizza uniform, over the head with her purse again. "You put that flyer back where you found it, or I'll report you to the police!"

The guy threw the flyer on the ground and took off down the block.

"That explains it!" Gabby yelled. "Presto Pizza is taking down all of our flyers because they don't want customers to go to Tony's instead."

"I can't believe it," said LC, picking up the flyer.

"What are you talking about?" asked Mrs. Crabtree, frowning at LC and Gabby.

LC and Gabby explained to Mrs. Crabtree all about the pizza war and Tony's problems with the bank and their flyer campaign to get business for Tony.

"*Harrumph!* Give me that flyer," Mrs. Crabtree said. She snatched the flyer from LC.

Then before LC or Gabby could say another word, Mrs. Crabtree strode away from them and headed for downtown Critterville.

CHAPTER 6

TOO MANY COOKS

On Saturday morning LC met the Critter Kids at Tony's. Everyone was there except for Gabby. LC wondered where she could be when the door suddenly burst open and Gabby ran in.

"You're not going to believe this," Gabby said, waving a copy of the *Critterville Herald* in the air. "This is way better than flyers!"

"What are you talking about?" asked LC.

"Look at this," said Gabby. She opened the newspaper to the second page. Tony and the Critter Kids crowded around to get a look.

"Hey, that's our flyer," said Tiger.

"Wow!" said LC. "Someone put a full-page ad in the paper for us!"

"I don't believe it," said Tony.

"How did our flyer get into the paper?" asked Gator.

"Beats me," said LC.

But before they could even begin to figure it out, the phone started ringing and it kept ringing all morning. Everybody wanted Tony's pizza. The Critter Kids had almost more deliveries than they could handle.

"See," said LC to Tony. "I told you it would work out."

Tony just smiled. The phone rang again. He picked it up. "What?" Tony yelled into the receiver. "When? Now?" Tony slammed down the phone.

All the Critter Kids looked at him, and even some of the customers turned around.

"Is it the bank again?" asked LC.

"No, it's my wife!" shouted Tony. "She's having the baby right now! I've got to go. I'll have to close for the day."

"But what about the bank?" asked LC.

"I have to go to the hospital," said Tony, talking very fast. "You tell everybody what happened, turn everything off, and put up the CLOSED sign, okay?"

Before anyone could say a word, Tony ran out the door without even taking off his apron.

"Hey," said Gabby. "I know what we can do."

"What?" asked Tiger.

"Why don't we run the pizza place?" said Gabby. "I can waitress." Gabby reached behind the counter, grabbed a pad, and stuck a pen behind her ear, just the way Tony did.

"I can waitress, too," said Su Su.

"And I can make the pizzas," said LC, tying an apron around his waist.

"Velvet, you answer the phone and take orders," said Gabby. "Gator and Tiger, you keep making deliveries. Timothy, you're in charge of the cash register. And Henrietta, you handle the toppings."

The door opened and some customers came in and sat down at a table in the back.

"Gotta go," said Gabby.

"Whaddya want me to do with the toppings?" asked Henrietta. She threw pieces of pepperoni up into the air and caught them in her mouth. "Yummy!" she said.

"Put mushrooms, pepperoni, and extra cheese on this pie," said LC. He pointed to a stack of pizzas that Tony had already made.

The door opened again and more customers came in.

"Hey, Su Su, you better hurry up," said

Gabby, running up to the counter. "I can't wait on all these tables by myself."

"Don't rush me," said Su Su. "I was just fixing my hair. I've got it all under control."

Gabby rolled her eyes. "Hey, LC, I need a small sausage and a small onion," Gabby said.

"Okay," said LC. "Did you hear that, Henrietta?" he asked.

Henrietta nodded as she put some sausage into her mouth. "Coming right up," she said. "I love sausage."

"Gator, here's your delivery," said LC, taking the pepper and mushroom pizza out of the oven. "Get the address from Velvet."

"I need two plain slices, two meatball, and one pepperoni," said Su Su.

"Did you get that, Henrietta?" LC asked, turning to Henrietta who was chewing a mouthful of cheese and peppers.

"Uh-huh," said Henrietta. She had little pieces of cheese around her mouth. "No problem."

LC started sweating. It was really hot working the oven. He wondered how Tony could do it all day long.

"LC, I need my pizzas," said Gabby, her hands on her hips.

LC opened the oven and slid out the two small pizzas. They were smoking. "I hope they like their pizza crispy," said LC.

"Those aren't crispy," said Gabby. "Those are burnt."

"Excuse me," someone yelled from a table at the back. "Is anybody going to take my order?"

Just then a long black limo pulled up in front of the pizza place. LC watched as the chauffeur jumped out and opened the back door. Oh, no, thought LC. It must be the bank. They must be here for the money.

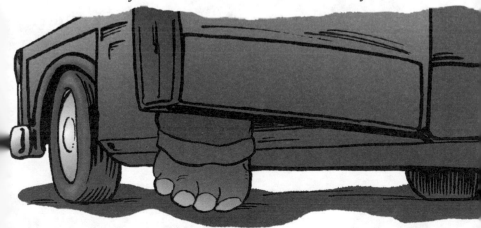

THE TONY SPECIAL

Marvis Bee walked slowly into Tony's Pizzeria, puffing on a fat cigar. He took a deep sniff and stared at the counter, right where LC was standing.

"Oh, no," whispered LC to Gabby. "It's the bank. They must be looking for Tony."

Marvis Bee squished his large body into one of the small chairs at a table for two in the front.

"I'll take his order," said Su Su.

LC and Gabby watched Su Su walk over to Marvis Bee, talk to him for a minute, and

then walk back toward them.

"He wants the Tony Special," said Su Su.

"The Tony Special?" repeated LC.

"Yeah, the Tony Special," said Su Su.

"What *is* the Tony Special?" asked Gabby.

"Search me," said LC.

"We should probably just put all the toppings we have on it," said Gabby. "That sounds pretty special to me."

"Yeah," said LC. "Then he'll realize how great Tony's is and tell the bank not to close him down."

LC turned toward the pizza rack. "Oh,

no, we're out of pies. I'll have to make one."

"Henrietta and I will handle the toppings," said Gabby.

LC started kneading the dough. It was a gushy blob. The more he kneaded it, the gushier it got. How in the world did Tony get it to roll into a big flat circle? he wondered. He decided to add more flour.

"What do you mean there are no more toppings?" LC heard Gabby yell. "Where'd they all go?"

Henrietta hung her head. "Uh, um . . . I ate them," she said.

"Now what?" said Gabby. "I know. Gator and Tiger, get some money from Timothy and go buy some toppings."

"Toppings?" said Tiger and Gator.

"Hurry up, you guys," said Gabby. "It's an emergency."

"That guy wants to know what's taking so long," said Su Su, walking up to them.

"Give him a soda or something," LC said. "We have to stall him."

Ten minutes later Tiger and Gator came flying back into the kitchen. "Here are the toppings," Tiger said.

Gabby opened the bag. "These aren't pizza toppings," she said, dumping peanuts, raisins, coconut shavings, and rainbow sprinkles onto the counter. "These are ice cream toppings."

"Well, you just said toppings," said Gator.

"It's too late now," said LC. "Henrietta, is there anything left over there?" he asked.

Henrietta looked all the way in the back of the refrigerator and came up with one piece of pepperoni, one meatball, and a few skinny slices of peppers and onions.

"Is the dough ready?" asked Gabby, staring at the strange shape on the counter.

"This is the best I can do," said LC. He

spread tomato sauce on the dough and put the rest of the cheese on top of it.

"Allow me," said Henrietta. She put the meatball, pepperoni, onion, and peppers on top of the cheese. "And now for the really . . . um . . . special stuff," she said, shaking handfuls of coconut, peanuts, raisins, and sprinkles on top of the sausage and peppers.

A little while later LC opened the oven door and took out the pie. He and all the Critter Kids stared at it. Nobody said a word.

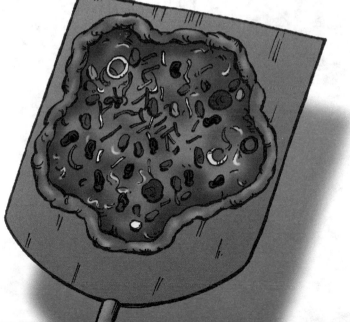

"Is my Special ready?" Su Su asked. "That guy has already had three sodas. He wants his pizza."

"I'll take it," said Gabby.

"No, I'll take it," said Su Su. "It's my order."

"You can both take it," LC said. "Just make it quick." LC watched as Gabby and Su Su carried the pizza over to the table. Marvis Bee looked up and smiled when he saw his food coming. Suddenly Gabby

tripped and knocked Su Su, who wobbled in her new pink boots and bumped into the table. The pizza flew out of their hands and landed right on top of Marvis Bee's head.

"Oh, no," LC groaned. "Tony's really cooked now."

Marvis Bee sat absolutely still and stared straight ahead.

"We're so sorry," Gabby said, picking the pizza off Marvis Bee's head.

"Here are some napkins," said Su Su.

"I'll get some water to wipe off your suit," said Gabby. She ran to the counter.

"Now what are we going to do?" said LC.

"I know," said Gabby. "Let's give him a free slice. It's the least we can do."

"Good idea," said LC. "But I don't know if we have any left." LC looked on the pizza rack and in the oven. He couldn't find a single slice of Tony's pizza anywhere.

"What's up?" asked Henrietta. She was holding a big slice with everything on it and was about to take a bite.

"I need that," said LC, grabbing the slice from Henrietta. "It's our only hope."

"Darn," said Henrietta. "I've been saving that slice for myself all day."

LC put the slice on a plate and handed it to Gabby. She brought it over to Marvis Bee.

"Here's a slice," said Gabby. "Compliments of Tony's."

LC watched as Marvis Bee stared at the slice. Slowly he picked it up and sniffed it.

Then he put it back down.

"Oh, no," said LC. "He's not going to eat it."

Just then the door burst open and Tony walked in.

"Hey!" Tony yelled, looking around. "What is going on here? I thought I told you to close for the day."

"Well," began LC. "We . . . uh . . ."

"He's eating it! He's eating it!" yelled Gabby, running up to the counter.

"We just wanted to help," said LC to Tony.

At that moment Marvis Bee stood up and began to walk toward the counter. A second later the door opened again.

"Oh, no," said LC. "Here comes Mrs. Crabtree."

"She must be here to complain about what we did to her pizzas," said Gabby.

Mrs. Crabtree marched up to the counter. Then she turned to Marvis Bee. "Well, Marvis?" Mrs. Crabtree demanded, tapping him on the arm with her umbrella.

"You were right, Eugenia," said Marvis Bee solemnly.

LC and Gabby looked at each other.

"What is going on here?" Tony asked.

"I would like to speak to the owner of this pizzeria," announced Marvis Bee.

LC gulped.

"Yeah," said Tony.

"In my entire life," began Marvis Bee, "I have never—"

 Tony took his keys out of his pocket. He handed them to Marvis Bee. "Listen, I don't have the money," Tony said.

"We didn't mean to drop the pizzas, honest, Mrs. Crabtree," LC blurted out. "But that's not Tony's fault."

"And we are very sorry about the mess we made of your pizza," added Gabby, turning to Marvis Bee.

"But you can't close Tony's down," begged LC.

"Yeah," said Gabby and all the Critter Kids.

"What are you talking about?" asked Marvis Bee.

"I don't have the money for the bank," said Tony. "These kids are good kids. They did the best they could, but it wouldn't have helped anyway."

"Would everyone please be quiet?" Mrs. Crabtree asked loudly.

"As I was saying," said Marvis Bee, "I have never tasted pizza as good as this in my entire life."

"Exactly," said Mrs. Crabtree with a big smile.

"Wait a minute," said Gabby, turning to Mrs. Crabtree. "Are you the one who put our flyer in the paper?"

"Yes, I am," said Mrs. Crabtree.

"And thanks to Eugenia, I would like to buy into this pizzeria and be your partner, Tony. Together we'll see to it that folks all over Critterville can enjoy your pizza," said Marvis Bee. "I'll start with taking care of your money problems with the bank."

"Yay!!!" the Critter Kids cheered.

"Hey, Tony," LC said, "did you and your wife have a boy or a girl?"

"A boy!" Tony said. "Pizza for everyone. It's on the house!"